Suddenly—

WOOOOO-OO-OOOOO!

A train whistle blew.

WOOOOO-OO-OOOOO!

"Hobo Dog!" a voice called out.

"Where are you going?"

It was Hobo's friend, the engineer.

"I'm looking for a Christmas tree!" said Hobo.

"Hop aboard! I'll take you where the trees are,"
replied the engineer.

The train roared down the tracks.

The wheels went *clickety-clack, clickety-clack,*

and the cold wind whistled through Hobo's whiskers.

There was the forest! The train slowed down.
Hobo waved good-bye to the engineer
and skied off to find his Christmas tree.

Some trees were too big.

Some trees were too small.

Then, deep in the forest,
Hobo came to a clearing.

There was a Christmas tree, just right.

Hobo chopped it down and slung it
over his shoulder.
By then night was falling.
It was time to head home.

But which way should he go?

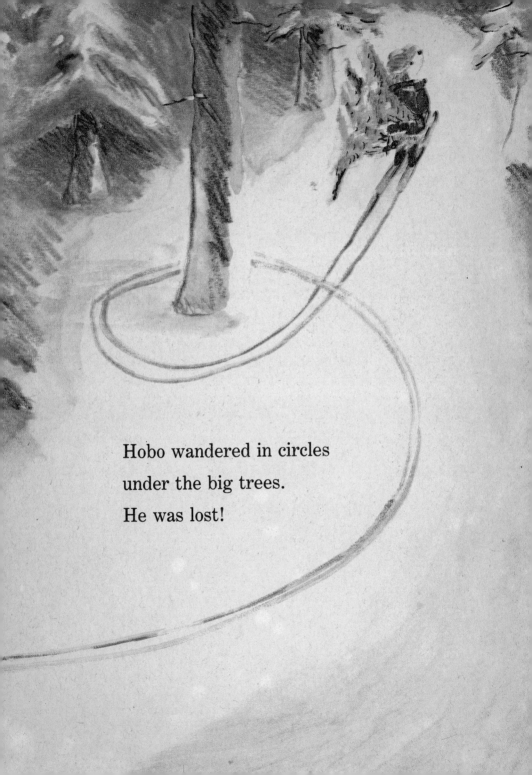

Hobo wandered in circles
under the big trees.
He was lost!

Then he saw a light, far away.

Soon there were more lights.

A town!

Everywhere people were hustling and bustling.
They were doing their last-minute shopping.

In a store window, Hobo saw a Christmas tree covered with bright decorations.
It had a star on top.
"I wish my tree could be like that," Hobo said.

He reached in his pocket for some money.
All he had was six cents.
That would never buy a Christmas decoration.
Sadly, Hobo headed out of town.

At the edge of town,
there was a steep hill.
At the bottom of the hill
were the railroad tracks.
Hobo started skiing down the hill.
Faster and faster he went.

WHUMP! Hobo hit a bump.
Hobo went flying, up, up, up,
over a fence and . . .

THUMP! into a snowdrift.
Hobo picked himself up
and brushed off the snow.

All around there were big shapes, little shapes,

strange shapes, funny shapes.

Hobo brushed some snow away.
A TV!

Hobo brushed some more snow away.
An old pair of shoes!
Under the snow,
Hobo found bottles,
tin cans, a wrench,
pots and pans.
What a junkyard!

And what a place to find Christmas decorations!

Hobo filled his pockets up
and headed back toward the railroad tracks.

WOOOOO-OO-OOOOO!

Hobo heard the whistle blow.

"Hop aboard, Christmas Dog!"

exclaimed his friend the engineer.

Away they went
down the long tracks,
the cold wind in their whiskers,
and the train wheels going *clickety-clack,*
clickety-clack.

Soon the train came to Hobo's little shack.
The engineer pulled on the brakes
and the train stopped.
Hobo and the engineer put the Christmas tree
inside Hobo's shack.

Then they decorated the tree with
all the junk Hobo had found.
"You need something for the top,"
said the engineer.

And he brought in an old signal lantern
from the train.
Hobo hung it above the tree.
"Just like a twinkling star," he said with a smile.